This book is gifted to

From

because you are loved.

For my mom, who has always loved me.
Special thanks to Sally Clayton.

# Did You Know That I LOVE YOU?

Christa Pierce

**HARPER**
*An Imprint of HarperCollinsPublishers*

Did I show it in my kisses?

Could you feel it in my HUGS?

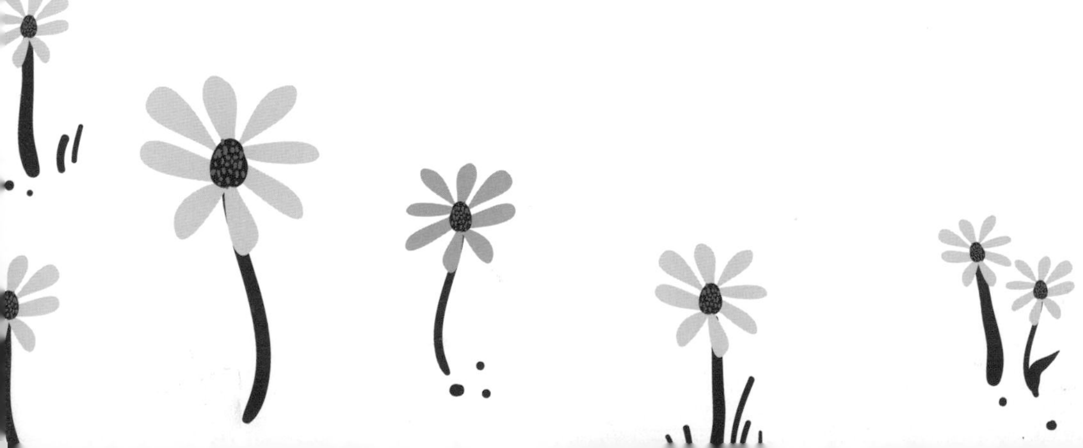

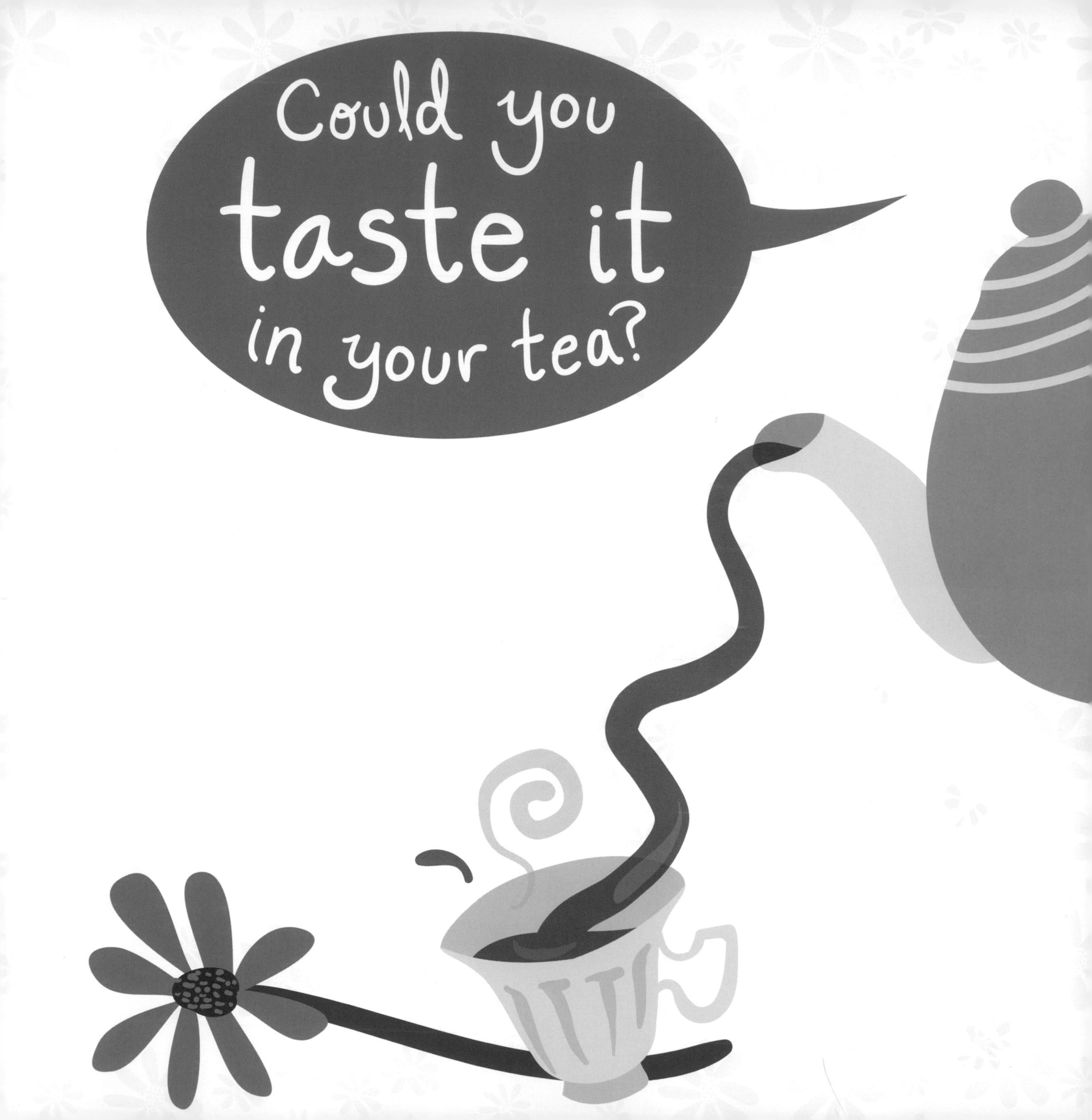
Could you taste it in your tea?

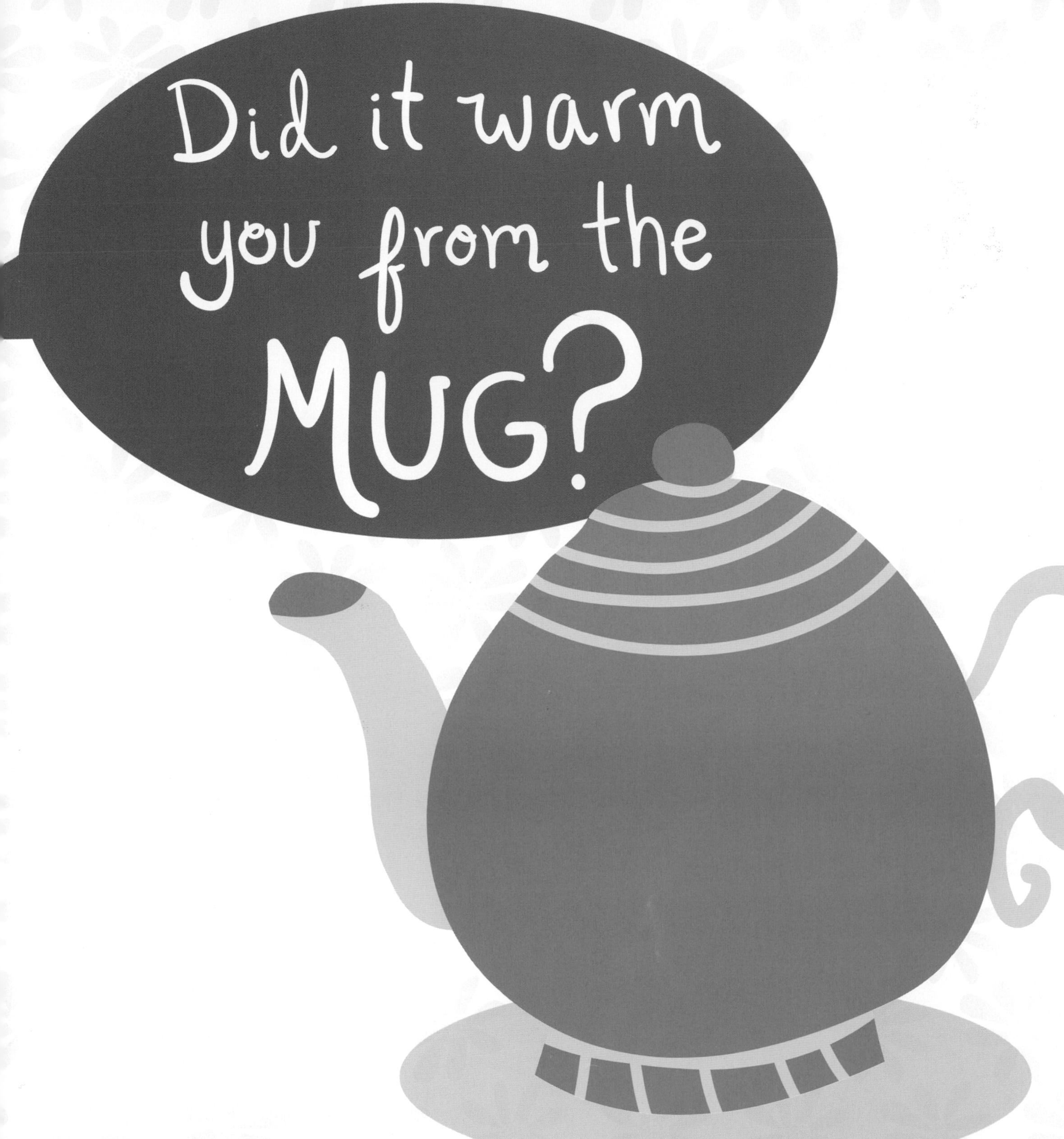
Did it warm you from the MUG?

Was my voice

your nighttime chorus,

with the rain
and chirping bugs?

Because
if you didn't know
I love you
I'd be really quite surprised.

I've written it
on the ceiling

and I've painted it on the skies.

I want you
to always know, however
big you get to be,

Did You Know That I Love You?

Copyright © 2015 by Christa Pierce

All rights reserved. Manufactured in China.

No part of this book may be used or reproduced in any manner whatsoever without written permission
except in the case of brief quotations embodied in critical articles and reviews. For information address
HarperCollins Children's Books, a division of HarperCollins Publishers, 195 Broadway, New York, NY 10007.
www.harpercollinschildrens.com

ISBN 978-0-06-229744-0

The artist used Adobe Illustrator to create the digital illustrations for this book.
Hand lettering by Christa Pierce
14 15 16 17 18   SCP   10 9 8 7 6 5 4 3 2 1
❖
First Edition